# Little Troublemaker
## Makes a Mess

LUVVIE AJAYI JONES

Illustrated by Joey Spiotto

PHILOMEL

PHILOMEL
An imprint of Penguin Random House LLC, New York

First published in the United States of America by Philomel,
an imprint of Penguin Random House LLC, 2023

Text and illustrations copyright © 2023 by Luvvie Ajayi Jones

Visit us online at penguinrandomhouse.com.

Library of Congress Cataloging-in-Publication Data is available.

Manufactured in China

ISBN 9780593526095

1   3   5   7   9   10   8   6   4   2

TOPL

Edited by Jill Santopolo • Design by Lucia Baez

Text set in Contemporary Brush URW

Art created with watercolor, crayons, and digital tools.

This is dedicated to all the future changemakers
and rebels with a cause.

It was a big night at Luvvie's house.
Her mom had a meeting to go to and Luvvie and her sister, Kami, were going to spend some time alone. No grown-ups. Just them.

"Luvvie, Kami," Mom said after she kissed her daughters good-bye, "there's some food in the fridge in case you get hungry while I'm gone. But I should be home in time to make us all dinner."

Luvvie loved her mom's cooking. The way the spices sizzled on her tongue made her whole body feel warm.

After her mom left, Luvvie ran to the kitchen and opened the fridge to see about that food. What would it be?

Leftovers. Luvvie's whole body drooped.

"Aw, man, I really wanted jollof rice!" Luvvie sighed.

"Yeah, Mom didn't get a chance to cook any," Kami said. "She's been really busy."

That gave Luvvie an idea.

"Wait!" she shouted, following Kami to her room. "We're not busy! Can we help Mom cook? We should surprise her!"

Kami shook her head. "No, Luvvie. It takes a lot of steps and it'd be a mess. And we have homework to do."

SPEAK THE TRUTH

"I finished all of mine!"
said Luvvie. "So I can do it."

"No." Kami closed the door in
Luvvie's face. "Go read a book."

"That's not nice, Kami!"
Luvvie shouted to the door.

Luvvie made her way to the kitchen. There was no way she was listening to Kami. And besides, Kami had just shut the door in her face!

"I'll cook the jollof myself!" Luvvie said. "I got this."

Luvvie grabbed her mother's apron and put it on. She grabbed a stool and pushed it toward the cabinets. She climbed up and reached for the ingredients.

"Whoa!" Luvvie cried as she wobbled sideways. "Whew! That was close!"

With her feet steady, Luvvie was ready.
"Okay, let's do this!" she said out loud.

Luvvie grabbed a butter knife
and began to cut the tomato.

The tomato went
everywhere.

"Yikes!" Luvvie said,
and then shrugged.

Then she grabbed the onions.
Her eyes started to water.

Squinting out of one eye, Luvvie poured the oil
in the pot, but half of it ended up on the floor.

"Uh-oh," she said. But she kept going.
Luvvie was not going to give up!

She grabbed some rice and poured
it in the pot. Well, half of it. The other
half ended up on the floor, too.

Luvvie looked in the pot. "That doesn't look good . . . " she said,
concerned. But maybe that's how it was supposed to look before
it got cooked?

It did have to get cooked, though.
Luvvie knew she wasn't old enough
to touch the stove. But Kami was.

"Kami! Come here! I need your help, pleeeeeease," Luvvie shouted. She was pretty sure Kami would be so impressed she'd apologize for that door slam.

"What? What do you want?" Kami shouted from her room.

"Can you help me turn on the stove?" Luvvie shouted back.

"Turn on the stove?!" Kami raced to the kitchen, and then slid over to Luvvie on a puddle of oil.

Catching herself on the
counter, Kami started taking
deep breaths and counting.

"What are you doing?" Luvvie asked.

"Trying not to freak out,"
Kami said. "But it's not working.
I AM FREAKING OUT!
What did I say about you cooking?!
Luvvie! This place is a mess!"

With her apron dragging behind her, Luvvie went back to her room. She felt just as crushed as those mashed-up tomatoes and wondered what she could do to make things better.

"The food is a disaster, the kitchen is a mess, and now we might get in trouble," Luvvie moaned. "And it's all my fault!"

But then she had another idea— if Kami was still doing her homework, Luvvie could clean the kitchen before she was done!

SNAP!!

"I can make everything better!" she said. "I'm gonna save the day!"

Luvvie quietly tiptoed past Kami's bedroom. She snuck into the kitchen and grabbed the cleaning supplies.

"First, the dishes!"

She got the dishwashing soap. She placed the dishes inside the dishwasher, poured in the soap, and pressed START.

Within minutes, bubbles began to foam out the sides of the dishwasher and flood the kitchen.

She began to panic. She tried to turn off the dishwasher. "OH NO!" Luvvie said as she tried to get everything under control. But before she could, Kami walked in.

"LUVVIE!" Kami said in shock.
Luvvie had made an even bigger
mess than before.

Then Kami burst
out laughing.

"You look ridiculous!" she said.
"I can't believe this."

They both started laughing.

DISH SOAP

"We have to clean this up before Mom gets home or we are in big trouble!" Kami said.

Right then, Luvvie and Kami heard the keys in the front door . . . Mom was home and was headed for the kitchen.

"UH-OH," Kami and Luvvie said together.

Mom stepped into the kitchen and her mouth dropped open.

The look on Mom's face made Luvvie's heart sink.
She knew she was in BIG TROUBLE.

Luvvie tried to confess, but before she
could get any words out, Mom said,
"What's going on? What happened here?"

Luvvie looked down at her
sudsy shoes and felt really bad.

"I was trying to make jollof rice for
dinner, Mom. I wanted to surprise
you," Luvvie said.

"Wait," Mom said, "you
tried to cook?? By yourself??"

Upset, she turned to Kami.
"Kami, did you know she was—"

"I told her not to!" Kami said.
"But she didn't listen, and I was
doing my homework."

Mom shook her head. "You have to watch her closely."

"I'm not a baby!" Luvvie told her, frustrated.

"I know you're not." Mom turned back to Luvvie. "But you're also not a grown-up. Your job is not to cook or try to run the kitchen yourself. You broke rules we put in place to protect you. Next time listen to me and your sister."

POP!

Luvvie realized her mom was right. She hadn't thought about why the rules were the rules, but she could've gotten really hurt.

"I'm sorry. I should have listened to Kami," Luvvie muttered. "Am I in trouble?"

"I'm glad you said that, and I know you were trying to be thoughtful. How about after dinner we can make a list of ways to make some good trouble?"

Mom reached for Luvvie and hugged her. "I love you," she said. "Also, you're going to help me fix this mess you made by cleaning up."

Luvvie was relieved. Even when she got in trouble, her mom still made her feel loved. "I love you, too," she told her mom. "Even more than I love jollof rice."

Her mom smiled. "Wow. That's a lot, isn't it."

Luvvie nodded. "So much. BIG much."

"Well, good news," her mom said. "I stopped at a restaurant and got us jollof. We can eat it after we clean up this mess. Deal?"

"DEAL!" Luvvie shouted.

With all three of them working together, it didn't take too long to fix up the kitchen.

Kami washed the dishes. Luvvie dried them. And Mom mopped up the floor.

Then they piled on the couch together to eat the jollof rice.

Luvvie loved every bite. "But it's not as good as yours," she told her mom.

Mom laughed. "You are such a little troublemaker," she said.

Luvvie smiled. "I am," she told her. "Sure am."

# What is jollof rice?

Jollof rice is a delicious rice dish that originated in West Africa. It is especially popular in Nigeria, where Little Luvvie's family is from. It's warm, comforting, and yummy! You can make it as spicy as you want. It has vegetables in it, and you can make it with fish or other meat. You can make it your own. Each family has their own special recipe.

# What is good trouble?

Little Luvvie got herself into trouble even though she meant well because she didn't think about what she was best at (NOT cooking dinner!). She didn't keep her own safety in mind. But there are lots of ways Little Luvvie could have channeled her good intentions and made GOOD trouble, the kind of trouble that helps our friends and family, helps our community, and makes the world a better place. Here are some ways to make that good kind of trouble:

**BE** your best self (and do what you do best!).

**SAY** kind things (try to be as thoughtful as possible).

**DO** speak up when you see something unfair (as long as you feel safe).